D0244475

700014517276

The
Three Little
Snowmen

There are lots of Early Reader
stories you might enjoy.

Look at the back of the book,
or for a complete list, visit
www.hachettechildrens.co.uk

The Three Little Snowmen

GEORGIE ADAMS
ILLUSTRATED BY EMILY BOLAM

Orion
Children's Books

ORION CHILDREN'S BOOKS

First published in Great Britain in 2018
by Hodder and Stoughton

1 3 5 7 9 10 8 6 4 2

Text © Georgie Adams, 2018
Illustrations © Emily Bolam, 2018

The moral rights of the author and illustrator have been asserted.

All characters and events in this publication, other than those clearly
in the public domain, are fictitious and any resemblance to
real persons, living or dead, is purely coincidental.

All rights reserved.
No part of this publication may be reproduced, stored in
a retrieval system, or transmitted, in any form or by any means, without
the prior permission in writing of the publisher, nor be otherwise circulated
in any form of binding or cover other than that in which it is published
and without a similar condition including this condition being
imposed on the subsequent purchaser.

A CIP catalogue record for this book
is available from the British Library.

ISBN 978 1 5101 0180 7

Printed and bound in China

The paper and board used in this book are from well-managed forests
and other responsible sources.

Orion Children's Books
An imprint of
Hachette Children's Group
Part of Hodder and Stoughton
Carmelite House
50 Victoria Embankment
London EC4Y 0DZ

An Hachette UK Company
www.hachette.co.uk
www.hachettechildrens.co.uk

For Mia and Esme – GA

HARINGEY PUBLIC LIBRARY	
70001451727 6	
PETERS	05-Nov-2018
£4.99	

Contents

Chapter 1

Meet the Snowmen!

The three little snowmen live in a very cold place. It snows there almost every day.

"Hello. I'm Frosty.
This is my pet penguin,
Poppet."

"Hi! I'm Freezy.
I have a baby seal
called Samba."

"And I'm Boots. My husky, Henry, is strong enough to pull a sleigh!"

Frosty, Freezy and Boots live together at Snowflake Cottage. They built it themselves. Instead of bricks, the friends used big blocks of ice.

"We don't need a fridge for food.
Our kitchen is as cold as a freezer!"

"Look! We keep lollies and ice cream
on a shelf."

"Fish fingers too. Yummy!"

At breakfast, the three little snowmen eat their favourite cereal, Freezy Flakes and lots of cold milk.

At teatime, they have iced buns with snowberry jam.

Guess what they have for supper?

Icebergers and chips!

Chapter 2
Holiday Time

At the end of every year, Frosty, Freezy and Boots go on holiday with their pets.

Early one Christmas Eve morning,

the little snowmen packed
their sleigh.

"We're off to the North Pole!" said Frosty excitedly.

"I can't wait to see Father Christmas," said Freezy.

"We must remember to take our stockings," said Boots with a smile.

Boots fixed a harness to Henry's collar.

The husky wagged his tail. He loved to race across the snow, pulling the sleigh.

Soon everyone was ready to go.

"North Pole, here we come!" said Freezy.

As they set off, it began to snow . . .

Henry sped away. The sleigh slid easily over the glistening snow.

Faster and faster they went.

Frosty, Freezy and Boots felt the wind whistle past their ears and snow-spray sting their cheeks.

Soon, the snow began to fall in big, feathery flakes.

The wind blew harder.

Henry pulled the sleigh through the snowstorm, even though he couldn't see where he was going.

"Where are we?" asked Frosty.

Freezy looked through the whirling snowflakes. "No idea," he said.

"Let's wait until the storm has passed,"
said Boots.

But the weather grew worse and the
snowstorm turned into a blizzard.

Suddenly Frosty, Freezy and Boots felt the ground move.

CRACK!

The ground shook and made them wobble.

"Wha-wha-what's happening?" cried Boots.

"Help!" yelled Freezy.

"Oops!" said Frosty as he fell.

When the friends looked around they saw
nothing but water.

Chapter 3
All at Sea

There wasn't much the three little snowmen could do but hope for the best. They drifted on and on for several hours.

The snowstorm had stopped long ago. The sky was blue and they could see everything clearly.

"Sea," said Frosty gloomily. "Sea, sea, nothing but sea!"

"I hope we're going the right way for the North Pole," said Freezy. "We don't want to miss Father Christmas!"

Just then, a seagull landed on the iceberg beside them.

She eyed their picnic basket greedily, then said, "Got any food? I'm hungry!"

"We . . . might have," said Boots slowly. "But first, can you tell us where we are?"

"Easy-peasy!" said the cheeky bird. "You're at sea. All at sea!"

"Silly bird!"

"We know THAT!" said Boots crossly.

"He-he!" squawked the seagull. "Only joking! North Pole ahead. Turn left at Whale Island. First right at the top of the world. You can't miss it."

"Thank you!" said Boots.

Then the little snowmen opened the basket and shared their picnic with the seagull, before she flew away.

Chapter 4

A Whale of a Tail

Freezy was the first to spot it.

"Whale Island!" he said. "Over there."

But Frosty looked puzzled.

"The seagull told us to turn left at Whale Island. But how can we make the iceberg go where we want it to?" he said.

"You're right," said Boots.

The little snowmen were wondering what to
do when—

WHOOOOSH!

A gigantic wave struck the iceberg. It tipped
everyone into the sea.

SPLASH!

Luckily for them, a whale swam by.

With a flip of her enormous tail she landed everyone on her back.

"Where to?" said the friendly whale.

"The North Pole, please," said Boots with a smile.

And off they went.

In no time at all, the whale swam to the top of the world. Then she turned right. From there it was just a short walk across the ice to the North Pole.

"No time to lose," said Frosty.

"Off we go," said Freezy.

"I hope we're in time to see Father Christmas!" said Boots.

Chapter 5

Where is Father Christmas?

The little snowmen soon arrived at the Winter Wonderland Holiday Camp at the North Pole.

There were log cabins around a frozen lake, lit by twinkling lanterns.

"Ooo!" said Frosty. "How pretty!"

The camp was full of excited holidaymakers.
That evening, everyone gathered round a
tree to wait for Father Christmas. He had
promised to be there before midnight.

People waited and waited. But Father Christmas didn't come. Some children began to cry.

"We want Father Christmas," they said.

"Hmm," said Freezy. "I wonder where he is . . ."

Then they heard a shout coming from the lake.

"HELP!"

"Follow me!" cried Freezy.

So everyone ran. And there, in the middle of the lake, was Father Christmas!

"We must do something!" said Frosty.

"But what?" said Boots.

The little snowmen thought for a minute.

Then Freezy had an idea.

The snowmen cut blocks of ice to make a path across the lake. The holidaymakers helped too.

Soon they had made a safe path for Father Christmas and his reindeer to walk on.

"Thank you!" said Father Christmas.
"My reindeer landed on the lake by mistake.
My sleigh is very heavy. No wonder we
broke the ice!"

"Hooray!" cried the holidaymakers. "Three
cheers for the little snowmen!"

"Ho, ho, ho!" laughed Father Christmas.
Then he filled everyone's stockings with
presents.

Chapter 6
Party Time in Wonderland

That evening, Frosty, Freezy and Boots
enjoyed the best party they could remember.
They ate delicious food and played games
in the snow.

And at midnight, they looked up and saw a magical display of coloured lights dancing in the sky.

"That's the Aurora Borealis," Father Christmas told them.

"Now, it's time I was on my way. I have presents to deliver around the world!"

Everyone waved goodbye as Father Christmas and his reindeer took off with a WHOOSH! – then up and over the moon.

"Merry Christmas!" cheered the three little snowmen. "Merry Christmas to you all!"

What are you going to read next?

Don't miss the other adventures
in the **Three Little series**...

Have a spooky
Halloween with the
Three Little Vampires.

Go on a magical
adventure with the
Three Little Magicians.

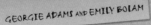